The New Teacher

Clare Helen Welsh

Illustrated by Colleen Larmour

Schofield & Sims

It was Anika's first day. Mr Montague greeted her. "Let me help you," he said. "This is your peg."

Mr Montague helped all the children.

"Today's first lesson is art," said Mr Montague. "Can you draw the sea?"

Mr Montague drew the sea with a blue pen. He helped the children draw it too.

But then Mr Montague's hand tipped up the glue. Oh no! Mr Montague was coated in glue!

Next, the children went into the playground.

"Let's do a few laps around the lawn,"
said Mr Montague. "Can you hop like
a rabbit?"

Mr Montague hopped around the lawn like a rabbit. He helped the children hop like rabbits too.

But then Mr Montague slipped and fell into the chicken coop. Oh no! Mr Montague had straw stuck to him!

The children rescued Mr Montague just as the bell rang for lunch.

In the canteen, Anika saw her teacher looking sad. Mrs Dewhurst went to speak to him.

"Is it true?" said Anika when Mrs Dewhurst had left. "Is it your first day too?"

"Yes," sighed Mr Montague. "And I am in such a mess!"

"You helped us, so we will help you,"
said Anika.

The rest of the day went much better, until...